No Place for Happiness

Scary Short Stories

No Place for Happiness

Scary Short Stories

Erika Lance

4 Horsemen
Publications, Inc.

Dedication

To every bump in the night.

Table of Contents

BITE

His mind raced as he feverishly knocked on the door.

When he had spoken with Alice, she seemed scared. He knocked again. No answer. He knew she was inside; he just wasn't sure what condition he would find her in.

Desperately, he tried the doorknob. Alice had never once left her door unlocked since she moved to what she always called "the big city." She had grown up in a town of less than 3000 people, so almost anywhere would fit that definition to her.

With only a slight turn, the handle twisted and the door opened.

Wes's heart thundered in his chest. He stood at the threshold of her apartment and stared into the darkness within. He realized he was afraid to take the step through the entryway.

Wes knew he was not prepared if there was something actually wrong. Most people were not. Some people, even in the worst situations, pretend that nothing happened at all, that life was peachy, that they didn't just run over their neighbor's cat.

As he began to create a scenario in his mind, that maybe she just needed rest and possibly ice cream, he released the breath he hadn't realized he had been holding. Then he heard a faint sob.

"Alice," he said, moving quickly into the apartment, through the hallway toward the living room. The only light he found on was a faint glow from under the bathroom door. "Alice," he said again as he reached the door, his hand instinctively going toward the handle. He tried to turn it. The door didn't open.

He put his ear against the door, straining to hear over the sound of his heart beating in his chest.

He heard the sounds of Alice sobbing. He turned so his mouth was only inches away from the door. "Als, it's me. I'm here," he said in the most reassuring tone he could muster. He heard the trembling in his own voice and hoped she hadn't.

He turned to listen again. No noise came from the other side of door now.

He tried again to no response.

He looked around. He had seen people break down doors in movies, but he wasn't sure if he could bash it in with just his weight. Wes scanned the living room and hallway then stopped. Alice wouldn't have an axe just lying around, and save that or a metal baseball bat, he wasn't sure what other objects might help.

He grabbed the phone from his pocket and dialed 911. "Als... Alice... I am calling the police." He was about to hit the call button when the door swung open.

Alice stood in front of him, and she looked feral. Her hair was disheveled, and her eyes were red and slightly swollen. Make-up ran down her face, and her clothes were torn and bloodied.

Wes reached for her and pulled her into a hug. "Are you okay?" he whispered. "Oh my god, Als. I was so worried," Wes continued as she leaned farther into him.

She was shaking, and he held her until she seemed to calm.

"Are you hurt?" he whispered, his face pressed to the top of her head. He had seen the blood and hoped it wasn't hers.

She began to shake again, more violently this time. She pressed her hands against his torso and pushed back. Her strength knocked him into the now open door, and he had to catch himself on the handle not to fall.

He looked at her, holding her hands in front of her chest, wringing them aggressively. Her eyes were wild, almost like a caged animal. "Alice?" he asked and began to move toward her again.

She met his gaze. Her eyes were completely black, and from somewhere inside her, he heard a growl. He saw something flash across her face before she collapsed to her knees on the tile floor, her breath ragged.

"I ... can't... breathe..." Her words came between jagged breaths as she started pulling at her shirt, tearing it and letting the pieces fall to the ground.

Wes didn't know what to do. He grabbed her arms to pull her to him again. *I have to get her to a hospital*, he thought. Whatever had happened, she was scared.

Before he could pull her all the way up, she tore herself from his grasp, again pushing him to the floor. When she met his gaze, there was a pleading in her eyes, her blue eyes no longer the black he had seen moments before.

"Wes, I am so scared. He bit me. I can't remember—he bit me. I can't..." Her words cut off as she began to sob again, her hands covering her face.

"Oh my god, Alice! Who did this? I am calling the police." He grabbed his phone again, and as he unlocked the screen to dial 911, she grabbed his wrist and shook it so violently he dropped his phone. He heard the screen shatter on the floor.

He was about to ask her why when he saw her eyes were black again. Her grip became tighter, and he felt her nails digging into his skin. He grabbed her wrist to try to pull her away from his before she broke it. "Als, you're hurting me. Let go! Alice?" he pleaded.

Again, there was a flash across her face and her eyes shifted. She let go and backed away from him slowly, looking at what she had done. There was blood running down Wes's hand. She looked down at her fingers with his blood flowing across them.

"You need to leave," she said, her voice flat.

"Alice, you need help. You need..." he started pleading again, getting to his feet.

Her eyes met his. Even though they were blue and not black, he did not recognize his friend in the person sitting before him. She had the same dark brown hair, the same pale freckled skin, same slight frame, but it wasn't Alice. Whatever she had become was now watching him, its head tilting back and forth slowly, studying him.

Wes picked up his phone and backed out of the room, shutting the door. He moved toward the darkened bedroom. He hoped he could find her phone on the night table where she normally kept it and call for help. He knew the only light in the room was a lamp in the shape of a fish her mother had given her when she moved. He smiled slightly, thinking how Alice would crinkle her nose when she spoke about it. He needed to get the police here. Alice had been attacked or raped or something; she wasn't herself and needed help he couldn't give her.

When he was almost to the lamp, he tripped over something large and heavy in the middle of the floor. His knees and hands hit the floor as he landed in something wet. In slight pain from the impact, he crawled the last couple of feet and pulled the cord on the lamp.

The light flashed on, and as his eyes adjusted, he found both of his hands were covered in blood. He looked down and found he was kneeling in a puddle of it. He looked behind him and saw the body, its face pointed in his direction.

"Jimmy?" he heard himself say aloud.

Jimmy was the guy Alice had been seeing for about a month. Wes had met him once when they had all met for drinks. He seemed like a nice guy and really into Alice. Wes was normally really good about who he got the creeper vibe from; Jimmy hadn't been one of those guys.

Looking closer, he saw that Jimmy's throat was ripped out. A picture flashed in his mind of how he first found Alice, and a chill shot up his spine.

He looked back to the small table next to the bed and saw Alice's phone. Frantically, Wes tried to wipe the blood from his hands onto his jeans. When they were mostly dry, he picked up her phone and dialed 911.

"911, what is the nature of your emergency?" answered a female voice.

"My friend is sick... And I think... No... I know Jimmy is dead... Please hurry... 438 Morning Rise Way, Apartment 2B," he said, the words tumbling out so quickly he hoped the operator understood him.

"I have police and ambulance on route. Sir, can I have your name?" she asked.

"Wes, Wesley Green," he said.

She began to ask another question when Wes heard the sound of movement behind him. He turned to see Alice in the doorway. A growl left her throat as she lunged at him.

He threw his arms up to protect himself as she smashed into him, pushing him into the table and the lamp. His head hit the wall with a sickening *thunk*.

His eyes closed as the world started to go dark. He felt a weight press against him. "Als?" he whispered. He felt her jaw close around his throat, and he could no longer breathe.

THE FIRE

Candace woke up screaming: "The children!"

This happened every time she woke from the same nightmare. It was only dream she seemed to have anymore.

She felt the tears fall from her eyes as she tried to focus on something else.

The sound of beeping was being made by the hospital monitors near her bedside. She wasn't sure how many were connected to her. The beeping had blended together in a white noise to her.

Her eyes were still covered in gauze so some light was pushing through. She couldn't tell if her eyes were actually open. She tried to move her head and felt a searing pain down her entire body.

Fire.

Memories flashed in front of her: the waking nightmare. The fire, the screams, the pain, and watching as the children were consumed by it.

One of the monitors began to beep more loudly. She felt like her breath was caught in her throat. She couldn't breathe. She heard the sound of doors slide open. A a soothing voice

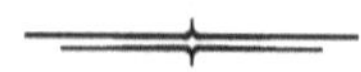

said, "Rest now, Ms. Westen," and she drifted into the drug-induced sleep again.

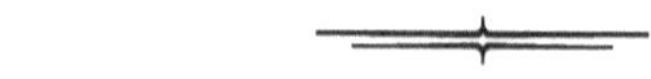

As she woke up, she heard voices.

"...they are still searching..."

"...guards posted..."

"...confirmed dead..."

She wanted to speak, but her throat was so dry that as she tried it was a harsh whisper. She couldn't form the words.

Her eyes were still covered, and as she tried to move her hand to feel what was blocking her vision, her arm only lifted a few inches. Something was holding her down.

She heard movement as the machines began to beep louder again, and her heart was beating out of her chest.

A voice she remembered said, "She is awake... Nurse?" It was Mr. Collins. He had been her mentor at the institution.

"Candace, calm down. You were hurt..." His voice was trying to be soothing, but in the mental fog, she continued to panic.

She heard more commotion in the room and then blackness again.

This time it was darker when she woke up. Her eyes were no longer covered. She took her time, breathing to keep herself calm.

She had no idea where she was, how long she had been here, and it seemed the times she remembered waking, she panicked, and they put her back to sleep. Candace wanted, actually needed, to know what had happened.

She licked her lips. They were cracked and her tongue was like sandpaper.

Deep breaths, she reminded herself as the beeping she had almost tuned out completely started to become more frequent.

She moved her hands around, feeling for the button. They always provided a button, and she needed a drink desperately.

Slowly, she felt around with her right hand. It was hard to move, as if her skin was wrapped in plastic wrap. In the dark, she couldn't quite see what held her. After a couple of minutes of trying, she didn't find it. She took a deep breath.

She then used her left hand which seemed to move freely, and she was able to locate the button and pressed it.

It didn't take long for a nurse to arrive.

"Good to see you up, Candace," the nurse said, then paused. Candace wondered if she was checking the screens. The lights in the room turned on, dimly illuminating the small space.

Candace tried to clear her throat, but with the lack of moisture, she started almost dry choking instead.

The nurse grabbed a pitcher to the right of the bed, filled a cup, and put a straw to Candace's mouth. "Drink slowly," the nurse said in a very soothing tone.

Candace thought the water would be soothing instantly. It wasn't. Instead it seemed to actually burn her raw throat. She did, however, take the nurse's advice and slowly sip. After a few minutes, it seemed to calm down, and she was actually able to speak.

"How long have I been here?" she asked the nurse who had been adding information to the chart at the end of Candace's bed.

The nurse walked up to the side of the bed, looked down, and said, "Almost three weeks." She seemed to be waiting to see how Candace was going to take this news.

"Three weeks?" Candace repeated.

The nurse nodded and then said, "Dr. Stamford will be back in the morning, and he will be able to answer all your questions."

For a moment, Candace wanted to protest, but she realized that the nurse, although being super friendly, was not going to answer the questions she needed answered the most.

"Thank you," Candace said.

The nurse smiled again and replaced the chart at the end of the bed, and Candace watched her leave the room. She was surprised that she paused just outside the door way and seemed to be speaking with someone. The nurse looked back for a moment and then walked away just as the head of a man that Candace didn't recognize was in the doorway. He looked at her and then turned back.

She heard the beeping on her monitors begin to quicken again. She closed her eyes and took a deep breath. She had to stay calm or end up in the drug induced coma again.

She must have drifted off again because she woke to the sound of a familiar voice. "Candace?" It was Mr. Collins.

Opening her eyes slowly, she saw that he was standing at her bedside.

She smiled. "Hello, Mark."

He smiled back. He had insisted she stop calling him Mr. Collins two years ago. She had a hard time breaking the habit but knew it meant a lot to him.

"How are you feeling?" The small lines near his eyes gave away that he was more concerned than he was letting on.

"Okay." She didn't actually know how she was feeling. "What happened?"

The doctor had not come yet. She also knew the doctor would only be able to explain the injuries and not what lead up to them.

Mark looked at her a moment and then walked over and closed the door. He brought a chair from the back of the room to the side of her bed.

She opened her mouth to ask a question and then closed it. The memories she had were fragmented and twisted.

"The children?" she finally whispered.

Mark's eyes seemed to turn hard for just a moment. He was holding back.

"Candace, do you remember anything from that day?" he asked. He was going to start where her memories stopped or were possibly wrong. This was a talent of his that he had taught her.

She closed her eyes and thought back to last thing she could clearly remember. She had been working at the institution for three years. Like so many in her field, it had started with a desire to help people and make a difference.

The institution had been born out of necessity. When humans began to develop enhanced or sometimes "dangerous" abilities and characteristics, it was found that normal facilities were not equipped to deal with not only the physical situations, but the mental ones.

It is known that most people cannot always cope when a loved one has something different about them. Disabilities have been scorned for years. Even with a growing acceptance and more parents willing to do what is needed to help their child, some were not.

Also, people with these mutations usually did not have others to speak with who actually understand what they are going through. It is very rough when you have something different about you that you don't understand and everyone can see it. You don't have time to come to grips with it yourself before you are being judged in the public eye.

This is most especially true with children.

Most with gifts that appeared at birth or puberty were also not able to control their powers. Most seemed to be fueled by a strong emotion. Fear and shame can be some of the strongest emotions.

That day she had been working with Noah.

Noah was an eight-year-old boy who had highly flammable bodily fluids. His parents discovered this when his diaper pail caught fire the third night he was home. They had him tested for everything under the sun, but all tests indicated he was normal.

The final breaking point for his parents was when he was five. They received a frantic call from the babysitter letting them know that she and Noah were safe but although the fire department had arrived, the house was still on fire. He had been moved to the institution that night. Although considered to be arson, it was decided to help Noah get his ability under control.

Shortly after Noah first arrived at the institution, there was an incident that happened in the boy's bathroom. Two boys perished in the fire and three others had been injured.

Noah said he had no idea what had happened and insisted he was being picked on and had run to the bathroom to hide when they followed him in. That the fire just started. He had received some small burns but was traumatized. He was then moved to the wing of the institute that held those cases that were deemed too dangerous.

Noah had been there for four years now.

"I remember I was working with Noah," Candace finally said.

Mark nodded.

"He was..." She started to say and then several memories tumbled in all at once. "He was telling me what actually happened in the bathroom... He was telling me about..."

"Elijah and Alice," Mark finished for her.

Candace closed her eyes. The images of the fire started to come back to her. The sounds of the children screaming. She closed her eyes tighter and felt Mark put his hand on hers.

He waited for her to be ready again.

"Are they...?" She started to try to find the words. They had been her responsibility.

"Alive?" Mark asked. She nodded.

Mark seemed to be collecting his thoughts before he answered.

Elijah and Alice had both come in at an early age as well. Alice was six and Elijah had been less than a year.

Both had what would seem like very minor abilities with unfortunate side effects.

Elijah could create a spark from almost any part of his body if rubbed. Like walking static electricity. His parents were young, still in high school, and they were unable to cope with his "issue." They couldn't touch their child without being shocked. This caused them to drop him at a local hospital, and because of the nature of his situation, he had been brought in.

Alice had not come to the institution until she was five. She was one of six children, the middle child with two younger siblings. Alice was not the only child born with abilities. Alice was a twin and her twin brother had the ability to create dancing lights. Her power, it seemed, was more ominous. She could cause all the water to be removed from an object.

When Alice was three, the family cat had passed away in the night. It was little more than a husk. They took Alice to a therapist believing she was unaware of her abilities. When she was five, her youngest sibling almost died. He was rushed to the hospital for dehydration which was causing organ failure. Alice was found in her room playing with her dolls laughing and smiling. She was removed that night.

Candace's memory twisted to the fire again and Alice looking at her from the doorway smiling and laughing.

"Candace?" Mark's voice cut through the memory and she heard her machines beeping again and the nurse was coming in.

"Wait!" she said to the nurse. "I am okay," she continued, forcing herself to slow her breathing.

The nurse looked from her to Mark. He nodded and the nurse left the room again, closing the door.

"What else do you remember?" Mark asked again. He wasn't going to answer the original question.

Six months previous, they had formed a small school type environment for the children. Building social skills seemed key in ensuring they were all able to reintegrate into society. If their abilities could be controlled, then the goal was they could lead a somewhat normal life.

It had seemed to be going well. There were eight students now. It had started with only two students with one hour of story time. This went well, and over time it developed into four "periods" where the children were learning everything normal students were, and more students were added in one at a time with Alice being the most recent.

However, as time went on, Noah, who was one of the first two students, became more withdrawn.

"Class was over for the day. I had asked Noah to stay behind. The children were gathering their things, and then..." She paused for a moment looking over at Mark.

Suddenly she felt pain shoot up her entire body. The flames, the fire, the burn.

The nurse came in again, but this time Mark held up a hand to indicate for her to wait.

"Noah?" she whispered between clenched teeth.

Mark narrowed his eyes for a moment and looked down. "There were only four survivors." He then looked up again.

"You, Noah, Elijah, and Alice. Noah is in the children's wing."

He let this news hang in the air for a moment as he indicated to the nurse that she should help.

As the nurse began to ready the next cocktail that would force her into slumber, Mark said, "They escaped."

"Who?" she tried to whisper but all went black.

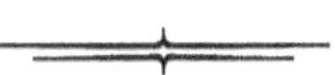

The dreams as she slept replayed the same moments over and over. The fire erupting, the screams, the pain, the helplessness.

Then the pain when she was awake was almost unbearable.

Finally asking for a mirror, she saw as much of the damage as possible without the removal of bandages. She was burned over much of her body, and the doctors said that the reconstruction was going to take years.

She found herself in tears regularly.

When she asked about Noah, she found he had less damage than she had sustained and was doing well. This gave her some relief.

She had been in the hospital three months when she woke to find Mark sitting next to her bed. He had a look of concern on his face.

He laid a newspaper out before her. The headline read "House Fire Kills Family." She glanced at the article and found that this was Alice's family and all had perished in the fire. They were still investigating the cause.

"We are trying to find both Elijah and Noah's parents," he said.

She looked up at him and didn't know what to say. "Are they together?" She knew the answer before the final words left her mouth.

"Do you think they are coming here?" she asked when he didn't answer the last question.

Mark folded up the paper and said, "I think they will come for him."

Candace tried to purse her lips and felt the slickness where her flesh was burned. She looked up at Mark and then away.

"We added more security," he said as he walked out the door. "Try to rest." She knew he meant for her to try not to worry. That wasn't possible now.

That night she woke when the door was opened. As her vision adjusted to the new light in the room, she saw there were two figures in the doorway.

"Alice?" she asked.

She tried to sit up slightly and reach for the button to summon the nurse. As she focused, she saw there was someone laying behind the two small figures: the guard.

"I'm sorry you're hurt." It was the voice of Noah and he sounded very sad.

"It's okay, Noah... Alice... I know it was an accident." Her voice was shaking as she finally found the button.

"Goodbye, Ms. Westen." Noah's voice again.

She was going to say something as she felt the air in the room go dry and saw a third head poke in just as the spark flew—the world was once again engulfed in flame.

A Simple Mistake

The clock on the wall said 6:47pm. Eight more minutes. She sat there watching. She always arrived with enough time to see the last moments.

The diner had been open for over thirty years. This wasn't the first time she had been called here. She sat on one of the vacant stools as the waitress took an order for a pie and coffee. Seemed like something that would be written into a movie.

Another five minutes passed.

"Hi," a voice said behind her. She continued to watch.

"Excuse me, Miss... " Normally she didn't pay attention to most conversations. They were never directed at her. She turned her head to look behind her and was startled to see a young man looking directly at her.

"Hello," he said. She turned and looked to see if there was someone now sitting behind her. Who was he speaking to?

"Are you okay?" he asked, looking directly at her. She was confused. This had never happened before. She knew he was alive. He was flesh and blood which meant there was no possible reason for him being able to see her sitting there.

She glanced at the clock: four more minutes. She also simply knew how close she was to the time of the event. Time was only used to measure the next event.

Turning her gaze back to the man in front of her, she noticed he was in his late twenties. He was twenty-seven. Again, this was something she just knew. He had reddish-blonde hair, and his eyes were teal. He was a little over six-feet tall and average build.

She searched him using her abilities to understand how this was possible. He had no magic and no marks of being touched by either side. What he did have was a sliver of a void on his spirit. *This is interesting.*

"I'm fine," she replied and placed a smile on her face.

"I'm Ben," he said and reached out his hand. She looked down at it. She had never touched a living mortal. She technically couldn't touch one. She looked back up at him. This type of circumstance had never occurred before. She wasn't sure how to react. She was unsure what his thoughts were, but he put his hand back down.

"I am..." she started, "not able to converse ... with you." She put a smile on her face again and then turned back to the reason she was here.

"I'm sorry. I just noticed you were a little lost in thought." Ben was still talking. She was soon going to have to handle what she was here for. How did she see mortals handle these types of interactions? She was running out of time.

"A different time," she said. Without waiting for a response, she nodded and turned to walk to the booth containing the mortal she was here for. She stood at the edge of the table. The occupants, a man and woman eating dinner, did not notice her presence.

The woman was talking as she cut another piece of her chicken-fried steak, dipping it in the mashed potatoes on her plate and bringing it to her mouth. The man suddenly clutched his chest. His pain would be extremely brief. By the time the woman noticed and moved to help her husband, yelling for anyone to call 911, it was done.

Taking two circular objects out of her robe, she placed them on the eyelids of the man. The spirit released and she reached to take what he would view as his hand. He let her.

Spirits were always very disoriented in the initial moments of their separation. The token or "coin" was the key that released them to disengage from the dead flesh. The coin also protected the dead flesh from becoming host to a myriad of creatures who would use it for their own horrible desires.

The dead flesh now in front of her was named Martin. He was forty-seven and married but did not have children. He had a defect on his heart that had continued to weaken as he aged and eventually caused his death.

She held onto the spirit. It appeared as if she was holding its hand. Sprits were so used to being in whatever body shape they were controlling at that time, they tended to forget they truly didn't have a form.

Ben was still watching her.

As the spirit's disorientation wore off, she projected from the restaurant to where she was taking the spirit. Projecting meant she knew where she was heading and could simply arrive there if she intended it.

She followed her normal routine, not giving Ben another thought. The spirit companion she had now was going to a hospital on the other side of the world. There a young woman was giving birth. He would be considered lucky by some as he had almost no wait to begin again.

The spirits didn't have "names," except in rare cases when they were stuck to long between journeys.

Most went into another life: whether human or animal. Others could end up as an object. It depended on the strength of the spirit and the type of existence they had. The judgement of whether a spirit was good or evil was relatively unimportant. Humanity needed both good and evil in the world for balance. This wasn't to say there weren't extremes. However, the accomplishment of survival was a base characteristic of the spirit. Without this, one couldn't become anything. She watched as the birth transpired and the spirit was drawn into the new flesh. It was done. She projected to the Hall of Waiting.

As she arrived, she became as real as a Ferryman could ever be. She needed to speak with Charon.

Charon was in charge of all the Ferrymen; he had been the first and now was the overseer. He created and trained the Ferrymen. She had only spoken with him once, the day of her creation. She had heard his voice and she knew her purpose instantly.

She approached the dock and waited. The dock was located in the center of the Great Marsh. This is where the rivers Styx, Phlegethon, Acheron, Lethe, and Cocytus all converged together and in this location Charon would come to find her.

Many thought that the voyage taken for transport was on the river Styx. This wasn't true. The rivers, all of them, acted as a holding place, like purgatory, for those sprits who were waiting to move on, were too "broken" to safely occupy anywhere, or deemed too dangerous to release. The constant movement of the rivers made it appear that there was motion. Therefore the spirits were not "waiting" as they were constantly moving.

Time also meant very little to the Ferrymen. It was measured by the next spirit retrieval. She had over fifty hours to her next retrieval. She simply stood.

It was twelve hours until her next retrieval when Charon appeared next to her. His appearance was that of a fisherman who always held his ferryman's pole. To a human, his height would be close to ten feet. However, very few spiritual creatures had only one appearance.

"κέρμα, this is a most interesting question," Charon's voice boomed within her head. She was unsure if anyone else could hear. He had called her by name. This was the second time she had ever heard it.

"Yes," she replied.

"I shall ponder this, and when I have a resolution I shall call you to return." With that, he was gone.

She walked back to the Great Hall. She sat for a time, and when she was minutes away from the next retrieval, she left.

She appeared on the edge of a rural road covered in snow. There didn't appear to be anyone in either direction. With only two minutes to go, she saw two deer walk out into the road. They were covered in their winter coat, a mother and foal. They stood out on the road looking up and watching the snow fall. They couldn't see or sense her.

Very shortly there were headlights, the squealing of tires, and she placed the coin on the forehead of the passenger in the car. The woman, the mother, would survive the crash. Her son died on impact.

She appeared with the spirit on the dock again and walked toward the landing leading to the water's edge. She guided the spirt to the edge, and it was swept away. It was to be contained there. In this last life, the spirit had caused the death of his sister and a friend. Both appeared to be accidents, and both died painfully, prematurely.

Four hundred and eighty-seven minutes until her next retrieval. She had time and went to see the Fates.

There were three Fates: Clotho the Spinner, Lachesis the Allotter, and Atropos the Cutter. They were three women who appeared at varying ages from young almost children to old and frail. They were always surrounded with what appeared to be thread. However, she knew they measured the lives of mortals.

There were many ways to find a mortal. Some were riddles to be solved, some ways were harmful to the mortal, and some had a price that was not worth paying for simple information.

She arrived and they looked at her in unison.

"Whom do you seek?" their voices asked as one.

She concentrated on his face, his name, and his spirit. Simply saying a name was usually not enough information.

They all closed their eyes, and she heard a sound like a violin string, soft at first, and after a few moments, it grew louder until it sounded like it snapped.

As it did, all of their eyes opened at once.

Atropos turned and pulled a small box from a ledge. All three women touched it and it opened. Within the box was a small cut thread.

"This is whom you seek," they said as one.

She looked in the box. This was impossible. She was of course not a Fate, but the strand was so small. It had to belong to someone who didn't even live past childhood.

"I don't understand," she heard herself say. There was no reason for the words; thoughts were enough.

"You will," they said in unison and closed the box.

At that moment, she heard Charon's voice boom within her head, "κέρμα, come to me." He could have summoned her to his side. He was her creator and had that power.

She nodded toward the Fates, who nodded back in unison, and the box appeared again on the shelf as she left.

Arriving again where the rivers joined, she found Charon looking out into the movement. She was quiet. Patient. She had two-hundred and seventy-four minutes until her next retrieval.

After a time, he pointed toward a crest in a wave. With it, he pulled a spirit from the river and willed it to the shore. It appeared to be a small child.

"This is James Michael Thompson," she heard him say softly.

Looking at the child, she judged him to be less than two in human years. The look he had on his face was akin to disappointment or confusion.

She looked to Charon.

"This is the human you know as Ben's twin brother." The voice turned to a vision. She saw twin boys playing in a park with their parents. The mother was blowing bubbles and the boys were chasing them on slightly unsteady feet. The father was smiling and trying to capture pictures of the two. The scene changed: it was night and the boys were sleeping in a bed together. There was moonlight streaming in through an open window. Then there was smoke, a fire, the children began to cough as they cried. It was the cries that woke the mother and father who began screaming. The father covered with a blanket that was beginning to char grabbed both boys who had now stopped breathing. The scene changed again: they were outside the house and there were many people trying to help. They were trying to revive the children.

Scanning the scene, she saw a Ferryman observing. She had seen him before: his name was *κύκλος*. He moved toward the children and pulled the coins from his robe. It had been too early. Both children were now considered dead by human standards, but the watcher did not wait. He placed the coins on James and pulled the spirit. Ben was revived. He had chosen the wrong brother.

"How could this happen?" She heard Charon's voice as the vision faded. This was what she was thinking. She had never believed that a mistake in taking a soul could be made. She knew that some of the more tainted spirits could put up a fight. She had seen this first hand.

She wondered what the next step was and of course Charon answered, "We have to wait." Looking down at the spirit stuck as a child, she wondered how this could be correct. "Jimmy, this is what his mother called him, can't move on until his brother does, and because his brother was supposed to have already been moved, we cannot see his death."Charon released the spirit back into the waters.

A vision began again for her. It showed different spirits trapped on what the humans called Earth. As the vision faded, she then understood now what these lost souls were.

It was standard that when she would encounter them, she would bring them back to the river. Now, she understood why.

She had forty-one minutes until her next retrieval.

She took another look at the river, focused on Jimmy, and saw him moving through the waves.

The next spirit was an older woman in a bed. Her frail form was finally giving out. The woman was surrounded by her loved ones, and with a weak smile, she took her final breath.

As she pulled the spirit and placed the coins, there was a sense of calm. This one as well would not be waiting long, and she took the spirit to a hospital not far from there. This was an old soul, and the community still needed her.

As the spirit entered its new vessel, the next retrieval time was set: twenty-one hours and eighteen minutes. She also inherently knew what she must also do.

Ben was sleeping now. She stood near in the corner of the room and watched him. This was what she would do now.

Ben finally passed at age sixty-seven. It was peaceful. His entire life he told those close to him that he had a guardian angel who was watching both him and his brother Jimmy. When

she had pulled him from the vessel, he smiled at her which she
watched until he entered the river and was swept away.

Do Zombies Poop?

I hate my job.

I usually go for a drink right after work to begin to relax. I find that if I go into a little hole in the wall bar, most people don't even speak to me.

Not today.

Today, I am seated next to Bernard. His friends call him Bernie, or so he has told me. Bernie works for the city in the Waste Management division. What does that mean? He is a garbage man. He must have just gotten off of work as well because I can smell a hint of his daily pick-ups in the air.

After spending fifteen minutes telling me about his job and some of the most interesting pick-ups, one which involved a blow-up doll, he asked me what I do.

I am an Environmental Containment Specialist, I told him.

He seemed impressed at first. I am sure it was due to the large words and the "Specialist" at the end. Most people think a Specialist means I am some kind of educated expert in my field.

That may have been the original intention of the title, but I have found that no longer applies. Instead, it is sometimes given to people to make them feel more important than they actually are: such as myself.

"Where do you work?" he asked. I sighed.

This was of course the next logical question; however, this was the part I didn't want to discuss. I looked over in his direction. He wasn't going to let this one go.

"I work at the Sunshine Containment Facility." I waited for his reply.

It seemed to take him a moment.

"You work with the ZOMBIES?" The last word came out more like the squeal of a child than the voice of the slightly overweight, balding man sitting next to me.

I looked over my shoulder to see if anyone else had heard this exchange. The last thing I needed was to have more than Bernie asking me about my job.

"Yes," I replied as I turned back to my beer.

"Wow. I bet that is awesome," Bernie continued.

I sighed. "I can assure you it isn't." I swallowed the rest of my beer, got up, and grabbed my jacket off the back of the barstool. Bernie turned. "Hey man, can I ask you something?" I wanted to say no, but some time ago I realized my response didn't matter. If I said no to that question, it threw almost every human on the planet off. They don't expect it. It seemed to have the effect of offending them at the same time. This usually led to more hassle than it was worth.

"Sure," I replied, sliding my arm in one sleeve then the other.

"Do zombies poop? I mean, they eat, right?" Bernie was genuinely interested in the reply to this. Most who asked this question were.

"No," I replied, threw a ten on the bar, and walked out.

I got into my car; it was about fifty degrees outside with the wind whipping around. It would be much colder by nightfall, possibly even freezing. As I pulled out of the parking lot and onto the highway that took me home, I had the kind of thought that I hated having after work. I wondered if all of the guests had been rounded up and put into the warehouse.

They didn't actually feel the cold. Or it did not seem to bother them. This didn't mean that they couldn't freeze. All flesh could. This would also advance the degeneration process.

I pushed the thought from my head. I wasn't paid enough to actually worry about this.

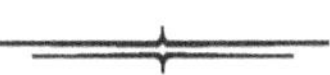

In case you were wondering, what is commonly known as a zombie does exist; although it is considered a slur to call them that.

About eight years ago, the first "zombie" was discovered. It was the six-year-old daughter of a family in Logan, Utah. Her name was Sarah.

Sarah had apparently died in a tragic drowning accident. Of course her parents didn't know this was the case as she was walking around. What caused them concern was when she ate the family dog.

The picture of Sarah sitting with the remains of the family's beloved golden retriever, Tinker, laying across her lap and the dog's intestine hanging out of her mouth is now the picture used as the cover of the "How to Handle the Recently Infected" brochure. I am not sure this was best choice.

Sarah's family took her to the nearest hospital emergency room. There was, at first, a fear she had rabies. If it was rabies, it would explain the behavior and the eating of the dog. It, however, didn't explain the lack of pulse and lungs filled with water.

The hospital didn't know what to do. Sarah couldn't speak; she seemed to only have primal instincts. The whole incident was kept under wraps by the government until a photo was leaked by the boyfriend of a nurse who had been bitten by Sarah in the beginning and began to change. Like any good social media addict, he took a series of videos of her decline until she was "removed" to the hospital to be cared for.

Her name was Julie.

The information was out, and at first the concern was about what this was. Was it a virus? Was this simply passed on by Sarah (aka patient zero)? It took the CDC about two years and many other victims that appeared across the country to figure out it was a bacterial anomaly.

In the exact correct circumstances, the bacteria would keep dead and dying flesh alive. In the case of Julie, it turned out that the bacteria fed off of the nutrients in blood and raw flesh. This was all she had eaten for several days, which caused Salmonella poisoning. She could no longer consume any other food or liquid. This in turn caused a fever, stomach cramps, diarrhea, dehydration, and eventually death.

It was discovered that this was all the end result of the bacteria begin injected into the system via a wound versus the bacteria lying dormant until a trauma, such as drowning in a bathtub, spurred the bacteria to kick in.

In case you are wondering, Sarah and Julie are both gone from this world.

Most people don't realize that a body exposed to air or water decomposes more rapidly. One month after death, a body can become more fluid and fall apart.

When they were first studying this "issue," the CDC discovered that the feeding on the raw, bloody flesh kept the infected alive. This actually prolonged their un-life so-to-speak. The more they consumed, the longer the bacteria kept their flesh alive.

You would think that during an outbreak of this kind, you would have seen a more decisive response from the government.

Developing a vaccine, for instance, or the willingness to put down the ones infected so it could not spread.

Unfortunately, none of this was the case. I think because of sweet little blonde-haired, blue-eyed Sarah, there was no killing. We as nation, and eventually the world, decided to find a cure to save these poor people.

So, what do you do with the infected?

It was determined to put them in Containment Facilities. This way your "loved ones" could be cared for while a cure was found.

The laws do not cover what happens if a corpse gets up and starts moving around. Half of the heavily religious felt this was a sign of the apocalypse. The other half felt this was a sign from God. Both sides however argued for the protection of these "people."

This is of course where the problem was: People.

You can't hurt a person. You can't kill a person. They considered these moving corpses people.

They needed to put them somewhere they wouldn't be a danger to themselves or others. It turns out the only real danger they pose was when there was fresh meat. Then they attacked. If they didn't have this to provoke them, they simply wandered around, stood in one place, or just leaned against things. They were fairly docile and just decomposed.

Since this was affecting less than .000005% of the population, it was not as hard to contain it as one would think. The first of the Containment Facilities was built in the Old Salem Jail in Massachusetts. That prison had closed in 1991.

Initially, this was considered a brilliant idea. In a short time, however, it became quickly apparent that the "Guests" (This is what they had started calling them) were deteriorating within the confines of this very dark, dank prison.

It was also found that in order to keep them fed, a Guest would have to eat about a quarter of their body weight in fresh meat each day. This for an average person was twenty-five to thirty pounds a day.

So, where do you get that much fresh meat? Of course, livestock was the immediate answer, but there wasn't enough to keep up with the initial demand.

So what was option B? Using the real dead to take care of the Guests. Yep. The government would pay you a fee if you were willing to donate your dead to help find the cure. That is how they phrased it at least. This became the main source of "nourishment" for the Guests.

This became a point that no one spoke of. The public didn't want to know how their loved ones were cared for, just simply that they were in fact cared for, or they convinced themselves this was what was happening.

Then about two years ago, it was agreed that the care for the Guests could be privatized. Meaning, the Blake Corporation was able to get the government to agree to let them build a state-of-the-art facility to help with the problem of different income classes of people desiring to have their family members offered a higher level of care.

The Cadillac of Guest quarters.

So, if you have enough money, your family member would be encased in a 10x10 oxygen free Plexiglas box. They were fed the best organic meat that can be found, and they were preserved twenty percent longer than other guests.

Then there were lower packages that could be had: shared accommodations or general population. This was where the Guests were in environmentally controlled rooms. They were able to wonder between these larger spaces. However, only a few of these rooms were actually built to stay warm. The thought was that the Guests wouldn't need to stay warm. Well, the weather wasn't totally accounted for. The Guests could freeze and then melt. So, this was not viewed well by the families of the Guests. It meant that the time that their family member had to hang on for the cure was dramatically shortened.

There was actually only one at Sunshine. It was called the Warehouse by the employees. It was where you could corral all the Guests so they wouldn't freeze.

People could also come visit their friend, family, or lover. These visits had to be scheduled because in order for the Guest not to be out of control and trying to eat their loved ones, they had to be well fed and cleaned.

It turned out Guests did not care about hygiene. This was probably the worst of the jobs at the Facilities. You might think it would be similar to taking care of those in a coma, but nope. Because of the nature of how and what they eat, they didn't care what kind of mess they made. Also, the fact they were constantly decomposing meant parts and pieces were falling off all the time. The oozing of fluids was the worst part.

So, that the visitors did not see was the plastic and tape holding their precious loved one in place.

Any people that came to work at a Facility quickly learned that any sympathy for the Guests was unwarranted. If you were here for some delusional idea you were going to help them, you would quickly learn you were wrong. Also, this new found knowledge could only be spoken about with other employees or the team councilor. It is part of the twenty-eight-page non-disclosure/confidentially agreement we all signed. It is iron-clad. Plus if you left, you knew how easy it was to "dispose" of a body. Did I mention you could not be positive for the bacteria and work here? Iron-clad.

So why did I work here?

I would like to say it is a funny story, but it is more pathetic then anything.

I was a Park Ranger at the Devil's Den State Park in Arkansas. I had gotten a Master's degree in Biology, which I of course discovered was a very specialized field. I didn't want to stay in school for my PHD, so I took the first job dealing with nature that I could find.

It was actually pretty fun. Sure, there were things to check each day, and every now and then someone would get bitten or lost, but most of the time, it was easy.

That was until four years ago.

Camping in the park was still a regular occurrence at that time. It was about two in the afternoon, and I got a call from Mark, the other ranger on duty that we needed containment. When I radioed back, it turned out that it was for two. By now there was a procedure for this to keep the person (aka zombie) safe and to have them ready for transport.

I called it in to the CDC and grabbed the two boxes of containment devices, heading to the scene.

Nothing could prepare me for what I saw. People say this phrase—I don't know how many mean it. I did.

"I think she was infected," Mark said, pointing at the male. I didn't know what to say. I actually didn't know if there were any words when you are looking at your younger brother with his intestines hanging to the ground.

Mark was still talking or screaming as I stood there. I just stood there.

I tried to close my eyes or look away or anything to not see what was in front of me.

It turns out the "girl" he was with was Megan. His girlfriend. She had been bitten by her father right before he had been taken away about two weeks before, and they were spending this last weekend together before she needed to turn herself in for containment. My brother was in love. I am sure he thought he had more time.

Jimmy, my brother, or what was left of him, lasted about two years in containment. I was able to see him most days. When the end finally happened, I was able to put him to rest. I realized in that moment that there was never going to be a cure to save the zombies, but the hope kept the Guests alive.

Sentry's Choice

C OFFEE!

That was his first thought and then his second. It was the only thought as his feet hit the floor to get out of bed.

The internal debate on whether to shower lasted three seconds because his stomach growled. He needed food as well.

Still wearing the jeans from the night before, he felt no need to change. He was not intending to impress anyone at the corner coffee stop.

He pulled a sweatshirt over his head as he trudged to the fridge to grab anything to stuff in his face and wondered what the day would hold.

It only took a moment of looking in his fridge to see that he was not a shopper.

He grabbed his keys and wallet and headed toward the door. He needed his coffee.

Benny's Bean Town was just around the corner. As he entered the brisk morning air, he thought about his meeting with *her*. It was scheduled for that day at 3pm.

As he stood in line behind a particularly anal person ordering the most complex version of tea he had ever heard, he wondered if he would be missed.

He finally got through the line and ordered coffee and a breakfast sandwich. At a small table near the front window of the shop, he took the first sips of the coffee and felt it warm his insides. His mind wandered to the events of the last two days.

His friend Collin had recommended they go to meet some "babes" on a break from their mid-term project. He was not going to argue an escape from the lab where he spent the better part of every day.

As he sat down at the bar to order a beer and watched Collin make his "move" toward some of the aforementioned "babes," he felt a chill run up his spine as someone took the seat next to him.

"You're Jimmy," he heard his new companion say or ask. He wasn't sure, but thought it should have been a question.

He turned to face her and was stunned. She was breathtaking. She had light blonde hair one could almost call silver and eyes that were a deep royal blue. She had pale skin and was wearing a black sweater and jeans. Her eyes never left his.

"You're Jimmy," she said again as he watched her plump rosy lips move.

It was only when she blinked he was able to realize he hadn't responded. He looked back toward the beers that were now before him. "Yeah. Yes... I'm Jimmy," he finally replied as he tried to regain his composure.

"Can I buy you a drink?" he asked as he turned to look at her again.

She smiled and shook her head.

As he studied her more, he realized that she was deliberate in her movement. Otherwise, she was very still in posture and expression.

"Jimmy, how is your project coming along?" she asked.

"It's good," he said automatically and took another drink. "Wait, are you in my Chem Lab?" he asked, already knowing the answer. She wasn't. He knew he had never seen her before.

"Jimmy, you should stop the project," she said, righting her head to look at him dead on. He felt the same chill again. *This is really weird*, he thought as he tore his gaze from the stranger to spot Collin across the room. He wanted his friend to look up and see her.

Collin was chatting and laughing with two girls at a high-top table on the other side of the bar. He didn't look up at all.

Jimmy sighed and turned back to find the girl was gone. He scanned the bar but didn't see any sign of her. He needed sleep, he decided, and took another swallow of his beer.

He had left Collin at the bar that night. When he met up with him in the lab the next day, Jimmy debated telling his friend about the encounter but couldn't bring himself to explain it out loud.

By the end of the day, he had convinced himself that he had imagined all of it and that he would need to make sure he didn't get that sleep deprived again.

Listening to one of his favorite playlists on his iPod as he walked home, the night air was cold against his exposed skin. He looked up to see the moon full in the sky. The walk was peaceful, and he began to relax. As he rounded the corner, he saw her waiting outside the door leading up to his apartment.

She was just as breathtaking as the night before. There was something different, however, and he could feel it in the air around her. He felt heavier as if he had been suddenly burdened with a terrible weight.

She gestured for him to lead the way upstairs.

He opened the door, allowing her to enter, and followed, closing the door behind them. He closed his eyes, his hands still on the door handle. He was obviously going crazy.

He took in a deep breath and hoped when he turned she would be gone.

As he began to turn, letting go of the knob, she spoke. "Jimmy, you're not crazy."

"Then what am I?" he asked, meeting her gaze.

She looked down for a moment, then back at him. "You're Jimmy."

She walked over to a window that faced the street and wrapped her arms across her chest as if she was getting a chill.

"What would you do if you were sitting in a bar and you knew the person sitting next to you would be responsible for the deaths of millions of people?" she asked. She did not remove her gaze from the window.

"I don't know. How would I know that? Is it Hitler or something?" he replied and ran his fingers through his hair.

"What if it was? What if it was Hitler? Could you kill him?" she asked, this time turning to meet his gaze.

"I don't know," he said looking down. "I... Why are you asking me this?" She moved and sat on the coffee table in front of him.

She seemed to take minute to gather her thoughts. "I am sorry, Jimmy. I should not have asked you that," she finally said in a whisper.

"It's okay... I mean, I would hope I could do something like that. It would be the right thing," he told her. He didn't know why, but he wanted to make her happy.

She reached out and took his hands in hers, studying them. "You're going to die tomorrow." Her voice betrayed nothing. "You're going to die because I am going to kill you, Jimmy."

He heard the truth in her words. They were not a threat or a warning; they were not intended to scare him. She was stating a truth.

He felt himself unable to disbelieve her.

Instead, he found that his head began to spin, and he was suddenly very nauseous. He closed his eyes and felt the world begin to tumble in around him. He felt his hands in hers again and knew she was the only thing that held him in place.

Her words engulfed him. "I thought I could stop it... Stop you."

"I'll stop whatever I need to. I will. I can. Just tell me what to do," he said, pleading but unable to open his eyes. He felt tears flowing down his face.

She let go of one hand and cupped his face, wiping his tears. He began to feel a calm seep into him.

"There is nothing you can do, Jimmy," she said, her words certain.

"But... Why?" He needed to understand.

"Because you will end up killing millions in the future," she answered.

"I'm not going to kill anyone," he said.

"Yes, you will," she said and blinked again.

"In eight years' time, you will be a very successful bio-chemist. You will work for one of the largest pharmaceutical companies in the world. You will realize, while working on a vaccine for hepatitis, that the project you started in your junior year of college holds the key to how to halt the infection of cells with the hepatitis virus."

"I will cure hepatitis?" he asked.

She continued as if he hadn't spoken. "It will be hailed as a medical miracle and the test subjects will show immediate improvement. The corporation will race to patent it and the promotion will begin."

"But... I..." he began again.

"Millions will get the new 'required' vaccine. Thousands will proclaim how it saved them. Then, an eight-year-old girl in Ripon, Wisconsin will develop symptoms that first appear to be a common cold. Her brain will swell with what the doctors believe is fever. Two days will pass, and she will begin to hemorrhage internally. As they race to save her, the surgical team will unknowingly expose themselves to a mutated strain of the vaccine. They will carry it with them all over town for days before they begin to show symptoms. This is the beginning. Because your vaccine halts the infection of cells, it will also halt the cells' ability to fight. Millions will die," she finished and looked away for a moment and then back again to meet his gaze.

Jimmy realized he was staring. He closed his eyes again and listened to the sound of his own breath. He felt her hands holding him.

Taking a deep breath he asked, "Who are you?"

"I am a Sentry," she replied, the corners of her mouth turned up slightly.

"A what?" he asked, confused.

"I am a guard. I am a watcher. I do not let things come to pass," she replied as if reading from text she had recited a hundred times before.

He was deciding what to ask next when she leaned close and took his face in both her hands. She pressed her lips against his.

It was as if he were freezing and on fire at the same time. It was the most intense experience of his life. As she pulled her lips from his, he opened his eyes to see hers sparkling as if there were stars imbedded deep inside them.

"I will see you tomorrow at 3pm. You should sleep," she said as she leaned in and kissed his forehead. He felt her lips long after she left.

His gaze returned to the mug of coffee in front of him and he realized that it was empty. He looked around the coffee shop at everyone going about their business, some enjoying their time, some rushing around, and it occurred to him that he hadn't even thought about what he should do before that afternoon.

Should I tell my family? Should I say goodbye to friends?

As thoughts began to race through his mind, it took only a moment for the calm to settle in, and he realized the only thing he needed to do.

It was 2:58pm when he arrived on the bridge. She had never said to meet her there; it was simply where he found his feet leading him.

She turned and extended her hand. He walked up and placed the notebook he had been carrying in her palm. He opened his mouth to speak, but before he could, she kissed him again. The same extreme sensation struck him, and he held on to it as long as he could.

His lips left hers, and he stared again into the starry skies of her eyes.

"Thank you, Jimmy," she whispered, smiling for the first time. Then he was falling.

THE QUICK STOP

PART ONE: HIS SIDE OF THE STORY

He was running so fast he almost couldn't breathe. His lungs were burning, and he knew his legs were about to give out. The *only* thing that kept him moving was the knowledge that if he stopped, he was dead.

The night had started with what he had believed was the same inevitable ending of every other night of his life. He would get off work at 2am, drive through the local fast-food joint for a dinner he would later regret, and watch shows he had recorded on his cable box. He would be alone, and he used to believe that was a horrible fate. Now, as he ran, for the first time he would have preferred to be alone on his couch.

Three days earlier, he should have known she was too good to be true. The first time he saw her, he thought she looked like a pixie. About 5'6", she had a slight frame and pale skin. She wore tight jeans that rested on her hips and a small black tank top that didn't quite reach her navel. He could tell she wasn't wearing a bra, but she was perky and firm enough to pull it off. He felt lucky the counter he stood behind was waist high.

He watched her as she moved in and out of the aisles and couldn't tell if she was wandering or looking for something in particular. Terror and embarrassment held him back from just asking.

He was staring when she approached the counter, a smile playing across her features. He met her gaze and saw that she had full pouty lips, light freckles, and a small upturned nose. It was her eyes that grabbed him though, violet encircled with silvery grey.

He realized that his mouth was hanging open when she giggled. He tried to compose himself by clearing his throat and scanning her items, placing them hastily in a bag.

"Hi," she said, smiling again and breaking the awkward silence.

"Um... Hi... Welcome to the Quick Stop. Will this be all for this evening?" he replied, reciting the same line he had said for three years.

"Yes, a... Jimmy. *That* will be all this evening," she said, looking at his nametag for a moment and then back up at his face as she handed him a twenty. He wanted to hear her say his name again.

He looked away. He couldn't seem to focus, and he didn't want to make a bigger idiot of himself by not being able to count out simple change. He tore the receipt from the register, counted back her change to her, and only when finished did he make eye contact again.

"Thanks, Jimmy. See ya around," she said as she left.

He sighed. He knew he wouldn't see her again. Most of his customers were locals or long-haul truckers. Chicken farms and a packing plant surrounded the small community of Clovertop, Kansas, and that was where most of the jobs were. The lucky ones, like himself, worked at the gas stations or restaurants located off the highway exit that ran through town. There was a small motel across the street behind the Breakfast Barn with only 12 rooms. It wasn't a place anyone stayed too long.

He finished his shift and went about his normal nightly routine.

He was surprised the next night when the pixie returned. She wandered again, picking items here and there, and approached the counter. She was dressed very similarly to the night before, but he noticed scratches on her left forearm.

"Hi, Jimmy. How are you tonight?" she said with a smile.

Don't stare at her he repeated to himself. "I'm good, thanks," he said and began to ring up her order.

Garbage bags, duct tape, cheese poofs, and an Amp Me Up energy drink. "Wild night?" he asked as he loaded the items in to a bag.

"You could say that," she said. Her hand brushed his when she grabbed the bag.

He jerked away, startled, and she laughed. He hoped it wasn't at him as he took her cash and made change. This time he handed it back to her without counting it.

"Thanks again, Jimmy. See ya around," she said again as she left.

When the door had closed, his head fell into his hands. He was a total idiot. With that moronic moment being his peak for the day, the rest of his evening ended uneventfully.

The following morning, he woke up and vowed to ask the pixie her name if she came in again. If he felt brave enough, he would even ask her why she was in town.

Before work that third day he showered, brushed his teeth, combed his hair, and picked out the cleanest and nicest jeans and shirt he owned.

At the Quick Stop, the clock seemed to drag on forever. He was trying to ring up a family, obviously on a road trip, with four children all under ten years old from the looks of them.

The kids were cranky and having problems deciding what they wanted. He didn't envy the parents. He almost missed the pixie when she walked in.

But she was simply mesmerizing each time he laid eyes on her. She began her normal stroll through the racks of snacks. He finally was able to ring up the herd, and she approached the counter.

He blurted, "What is your name?" He had hoped to be more eloquent, but at least he managed to ask her.

She smiled and tilted her head. "My name is Willow."

He rang up her items with a satisfied smile on his face.

"Jimmy, do you want to hang out later?" Willow asked as he was handing her back the change.

He froze. That was the first time a girl had asked him out and he was at a total loss.

Ignoring his silence, she said, "Well, if you want to, hang out that is, pick me up after your shift. I am in room 6 at the motel." She grabbed the bag off the counter.

He nodded, still unable to speak.

"Thanks again, Jimmy. See ya soon." She winked at him as she left.

———✦———

Part 2: Her Side of the Story

She couldn't remember the last time she woke up and knew the name of the town or city she was in.

Everything had changed the year before when Thorn had gotten sick. Sometimes she wondered if the method of keeping him alive was worth the cost. There had to be a cure. She couldn't lose him.

They had arrived in Clovertop to simply fill up and move on. Usually smaller towns weren't able to provide what Thorn needed. She was filling up the tank on the truck when the bed moved. Thorn was awake. Since it wasn't nighttime, she didn't know how it was possible, unless he sensed food.

She looked around at the depressing excuse that was being called a town. It was nothing but gray, and she couldn't imagine what he sensed, maybe a traveler like themselves. Then she saw it: a faint wisp leading into a store in front of her. She looked at the sign, *The Quick Stop*. Closing her eyes, she took a deep breath and *looked* at the people in the store.

It was strong. The spirit that was emanating the mist was not in the store then, but was there regularly. She could sense it all around. She would wait. The truck bed moved again as Thorn struggled against his confinement. It had been too long since he had eaten.

She spotted a motel across the street and headed across to get a room.

The distance from the motel to the *Quick Stop* was enough that if Thorn was sensing the spirit she couldn't tell. As she sat with him and waited, wanting to be sure of her perceptions, he seemed dormant again so she headed back across the street.

When she walked in, she could feel it all around her, caressing her skin as if she was in a warm bath. She looked around and found the source. Behind the counter stood the clerk, and he was staring at her.

She looked away, not wanting to seem obvious, and gathered up the supplies she need for the night.

As she approached the counter she studied her find. Nothing if not ordinary, he was average height with an average build. His short dark brown hair and brown eyes would never set him apart. He looked about 20 years old, but she had to be sure he was what he appeared. She couldn't afford to make another mistake.

It would take three turns of the sun to know for sure. He was worth it.

When she returned to the room, she saw Thorn had whipped himself into a frenzy. Three nights, she told him as she forced him into the quiet.

She began the spells that night, taking each layer apart. It took time and most of her power. She was exhausted, and each night when Jimmy showed up to work, Thorn became worse.

She had to resort to locking him down in the bathroom. On the last night, she was as sure as she could be. She took Thorn to a clearing in the woods behind the motel and bound him enough that he wouldn't be able to wander but not enough to keep him contained once he caught the scent.

She went to the Quick Stop, and Jimmy asked her name. She willingly gave it. He didn't know how to use it to hurt her and soon enough it wouldn't matter. She invited him out and with a little word of suggestion knew he would arrive.

She opened the door before he even had a chance to knock. He seemed surprised, even more so when she planted a soft kiss on his lips. He smiled euphorically when she pulled away. She took his hand in hers and led him down behind the building.

Jimmy was happier then he would ever be in his life. Her kiss had ensured that. She couldn't change what was about to happen, but she could give him that.

As she neared the clearing, she heard the sounds of Thorn's bonds tearing. "I'm sorry," she whispered to Jimmy's smiling face and then was gone.

Jimmy found himself standing alone in the clearing behind the motel. He looked around, confused.

"Willow? Where did you go?" he called. He heard a noise crash through the trees in front of him.

A creature emerged. It looked like something out of a nightmare. Its skin was a sickly green where it wasn't falling off the bone, and in the sunken eye sockets were yellow globes where eyes should have been. When it opened its mouth, sharp broken teeth lined the gums. It made a noise akin to a scream. Then the stench hit Jimmy. All he could think was, *RUN!*

As he tore through the trees he didn't look back. Jimmy could hear it breathing behind him. *Keep running*, he repeated. His lungs were burning and his legs were growing numb when the worst happened.

His foot snagged on a tree root, and he tumbled to the ground. Within seconds, the creature was on him, tearing at his chest. He closed his eyes. He could scream, but he knew no one would hear, and it wouldn't change what was about to happen.

Jimmy focused on the tingling in his lips and the memory of her kiss. It only hurt for a moment when his rib cage was ripped open and his heart was yanked from his chest.

Willow sat on a branch, watching the scene unfold beneath her. She floated to the ground as Thorn drank in the essence from the flesh he now held.

Jimmy's innocence fed the stricken Fae, and for a minute, Thorn's grey-green eyes met hers. She smiled and gently caressed his cheek. He raised his blood coated hand to hers and closed his eyes.

THE SUNDRESS

The day begins again.

The morning light is playing across the light blue curtains that are rustling in the breeze. I chose those curtains because they remind me of the bluest of skies on a summer day. It doesn't hurt that they match perfectly with the white panel walls of the bedroom. They are not thick enough to block out the sun in the morning or hold back the wind from the open window, which makes them perfect.

I stretch out on the comfy bed that used to belong to my great grandmother. Well, the frame belonged to her; the mattress is new and is absolutely comfortable to cuddle on. The quilt that covers the bed was my grandmother's. She gave it to me on my 16th birthday.

My mother is a big fan of antique farmhouse furniture. She loves to browse through antique shops for hours. When I was younger, I used to go with her. She loved telling me all about the different pieces. I think she relished the moments of life the items must have witnessed.

As I look around my room, I see all of those moments, both familial and my own. I can't help but think how my mother finds each one to be a treasure. She had hand painted small flowers just under the shelf that circles my entire room. It is about a foot from the ceiling and holds all kinds of toys, books, and pictures from my life starting when I was a small child.

I finally get myself out of bed after one last long, good stretch.

I look around the room and can't help but think about how it is the little things you look back on in life. I wonder how often people think that they should pay more attention to them. There is a card, for instance, that sits on my dresser mirror and is surrounded by the pictures of my friends old and new. It was given to me in the 7th grade by Jason Masterson. He was the cutest boy in my class. The card is shaped like a pink candy heart with the words "Be Mine" on the front. Inside it reads, "Will you be my Valentine?" and is signed "Jason."

I remember that day being one of the most amazing days of my life at that point.

It didn't work out with Jason and me. Most middle school relationships don't seem to last more than a few weeks, though ours lasted until summer when his parents sent him to a camp in Florida. It was a long way from South Carolina. After a month of not talking, I think we both knew it was over.

He had the prettiest light blue eyes, like the sky in summertime.

He went to a different high school than mine, but we've run into each other a few times since then. He would always smile when he saw me, and we would hug like old friends. It always made me happy that we never promised to call each other; we knew we wouldn't follow through. I never told him that I still had the card.

I put the card back on the dresser, pull off my pajama top and shorts, and place them at the foot of the bed before I head into the bathroom.

I take a longer shower. It is Saturday, and I'm not in any rush. It's nice when you are not under a tight deadline to be somewhere and can take time for you.

As I stand under the heated water cascading down on me, I can't help but get a little excited about what the rest of the day will hold. I always feel this way when I picture seeing him.

Patrick is one of the best things to ever happen to me. He's smart, funny, and best of all has a very cute dimple when he smiles.

We met at the local county fair. I was playing the ball toss, the one into the goldfish bowls. I was terrible at it, but Patrick swooped in and was my "Goldfish Hero" and won me not only one, but three of the tiny fishes. Not that I had any idea what in the world I would do with three goldfish in very un-naturally colored water.

He stood just over six feet tall with dark wavy hair and brown eyes. He was wearing jeans, sneakers, and a light brown t-shirt with a pocket on the left side of his chest. It was a little tight, and I could see that he had a muscular build.

His only demand when he presented me with the fishy prize was to know my name. My friends were giggling and teasing me the whole time. With flushed cheeks, I told him my name was Ronnie. It is Veronica, which he of course knows now, but I like being called Ronnie because my grandmother is also Veronica.

Patrick smiled as he presented me with the fish and said, "I look forward to bumping into you again, Ronnie" before he turned and began to walk away. My friends and I turned to head in the opposite direction. I was a little disappointed that I would only have the fish to remember the encounter when he turned and shouted, "I work at the Gas Stop on Route 22 in case you were wondering where to bump into me."

It took me about three weeks to "bump" into him again. I went to the Gas Stop four times, but he wasn't there until the last trip. He was behind the counter, and I was able to see him through the window before he saw me.

He was helping a customer when I walked in. The door chimed as I entered and he looked up. When he met my gaze, he smiled. "Took you long enough," he greeted as he finished up with the customer, and I approached him at the counter.

We talked for a little while between customers, and he asked if he could take me out sometime. I, of course, tried to play a little coy, but that only works when you don't drive out to a gas station on the outskirts of town to "bump" into someone.

He took me out for a picnic that weekend. It was up near the lakeshore, a perfect spot under the shade of a huge tree with a perfect view. I remember it was a little chilly out that day. I had dressed to look cute, not taking the weather into account.

As the wind picked up, my teeth started to chatter, and I tried, unsuccessfully, to hide it. Patrick noticed though and took off his jacket, wrapping it around me. If I had read our date in a romance novel, I would have thought it would not ever have ever happened in real life. It was perfect.

From that moment on, I knew that Patrick had my heart.

It turned out Patrick was in school like me. His major was English Literature, and he wanted to one day teach and inspire young writers. Sometimes we would cuddle in the hammock in my backyard, and I would fall asleep in his arms listening to him read me whatever novel he was in the middle of at the time.

After the water starts to cool in the shower, I wrap myself in a fluffy towel and wipe away the steam on the mirror. It has been one year since our first date. My hair is longer now and also lighter, almost a white blonde in some places from being outside so much. My skin has tanned a little, but I can still see all the little freckles on my nose that Patrick loves second only to my lips.

This thought makes me smile a little, and I find my fingers instinctively touching my lips, gently remembering the last time we kissed.

I head to my closet and pick out a dress I had purchased last week. It's a light yellow sundress with little daisies around the hem. I almost didn't try it on because the flowers seemed a little tacky, but my friend Beth had insisted. When I walked out of the dressing room with it on, Beth's mouth opened and then she smiled. She didn't have to say anything; I knew this was the dress for today.

As I put it on and strap on my sandals, I look at the clock on my nightstand. I have only a couple of minutes before he arrives, and I start to feel butterflies in my stomach. All of my friends say that feeling fades over time; I hope they are wrong.

I put on the necklace Patrick gave me for Valentine's Day. It's silver with three small heart pendants. As I clasp it around my neck, I hear the doorbell ring.

I grab my sweater and head down the stairs. As I hit the last few steps, I see my mother has greeted him at the door. She's telling him about the cobbler she is planning to make tomorrow night for dinner, which he is of course invited to. He thanks her just as his eyes meet mine.

Butterflies.

I reach the foyer, and he tells me that I look wonderful. He shudders slightly, and I know I chose the right dress. There is nothing like taking someone's breath away. He helps me with my sweater, and my mother tells us to have fun.

He drives us to the spot where we had our first date. He lays out the blanket for us and sets out another wonderful meal. We eat and talk. The wind is rustling the trees with a perfect breeze. We end up sitting close, looking out at the lake, his arm around me and my head on his shoulder.

I look up at him and say, "I want to come here every year with you, forever." He kisses me lightly and nods his head. "Me too," he says.

We hear the squealing of tires and a loud crack. As we turn, we see a pick-up truck barreling toward us. I have no time to move as I feel it hit me, and I am flying.

I think I black out because the next moment I am looking down from the picnic spot. Patrick is laying to my right. His neck is at a weird angle, not moving.

I hear a scream as I turn my head to peer down at the truck. Its front end is in the water. Just beneath the surface, I see light yellow fabric with little white daisies.

The day begins again.

TICKLE TICKLE

 thought you said this was a 'large' cottage," Veronica Niles said to the realtor as she looked at the house in front of her, peering over her Armani sunglasses.

Mari laughed the way a person does to humor a person, not that what the person said was genuinely funny.

"And the color is horrible," Veronica continued.

Mari, a realtor in the Millstown area for five years, was very used to dealing with people like Veronica Niles. Rich and pretentious, they always expected the vacation homes they were looking at to be something out of Lifestyles of the Rich and Famous versus the cute cottages that were the majority of what occupied the quaint sea side town of Thistle Harbor, the now "in" spot to have a vacation home.

"Why don't we take a look inside?" Mari said to the couple and began to walk up the stairs leading to the wraparound porch. This was one of the most attractive of the cottages still left on the market.

Mari opened the door and stepped aside to let the Niles walk in front of her. Veronica Niles was in her late forties, although the cosmetic surgery team that worked on her kept most of her looking perfectly plastic. She was about 5'4 but wore stiletto heels that Mari was sure cost more than a weeks' worth of her own salary. Veronica kept her blonde hair, not natural, in a tight ponytail and held her designer purse with perfectly manicured hands. She was a walking designer label stereotype.

Mr. Niles, or Robert as he insisted, was in his late fifties and bald. His tan came from a booth. Just shy of 5'7" he was towered over by his wife, which was evident in more than just height.

Mari showed the couple around the house. She told them every detail of the construction, including the newest additions of skylights and a pool, which many of the homes in the area didn't possess.

As they entered the sunroom that looked out over the bay, Victoria's shrill voice cut the air. "What the hell is that thing?" she said cringing and pointing at something crumpled in the corner of the room.

Mari glanced over to the corner at what looked like a pile of rags. Mari closed her eyes and took a steadying breath. This was the part she had always hated when she showed the house. Sometimes she was lucky and the prospective buyers would not even see it. Then, when she did her required "disclosure," it just sounded like a silly story.

Mari turned to the couple. Clasping her hands in front of her, she began to speak without making eye contact. "That is Rosey. It is a doll left from the original owner of this house." She paused for only a beat before resuming, "Over 100 years ago this house was built by Mr. Steven Standon. Mr. Standon built many of the seaside cottages, mainly to lure better skilled labor to his fishery. One of the families that came were the Miltons. The Miltons had a daughter named Rose. Mr. Standon took, let's just say, an unhealthy interest in Rose, given her age of eight. Things such as this were hardly spoken of back then, but Mr. Milton confronted Mr. Standon in public after his daughter told him that Mr. Standon had played the 'tickle game' with her.

Two days later, there was an accident, and Mr. Milton died at the fishery. Mrs. Milton, distraught and ashamed, took her life. Rose was found over a week after her mother had hung herself, alone in the house with her mother's body. Rose was made a ward of the state and little else is known about what happened to her. When the house was restored years later, that doll was found inside. Every person who has owned this house that has tried to dispose of that doll has had a tragic accident or worse."

When Mari finished, she looked into the very annoyed face of Mrs. Veronica Niles. "Are you trying to say that the house is haunted by a doll?" When the last word left her mouth, she began to make a noise Mari could only put in the category of a cackle. The irony of her sounding like a wicked witch from a fairytale was not lost on Mari.

"I was merely giving the required disclaimer." Mari straightened her stance. "The current owners wanted to ensure that outside of the disclaimer of a crime that is required by the state that any new potential owners were warned about the doll and the ramifications of its attempted removal," Mari finished.

Veronica made a noise and waved her hand in front of Mari as if waving her off like some small bug.

Mari smiled her well-practiced fake smile and walked toward the kitchen, glancing back to where the doll lay and said, "Please let me know if you have any further questions. I will be in the kitchen." Again, Veronica waved her away and Mr. Niles continued to look out at the pool area and the view beyond.

After about fifteen minutes, Mr. Niles came into the kitchen and told Mari that they would be in touch.

Before Mari left, she made one last circuit through the house. Although she didn't like being alone in the house, it was her responsibility to make sure that the premises were secure.

When she got to the back porch, she heard the crack of thunder and saw storm clouds off in the distance. She looked over at the doll in the corner. If it stayed outside, it would be ruined. The moment she thought that she wished she hadn't. She turned to walk away, feeling that if she didn't get involved at all, it would be better. She took a tentative step, and then realized she needed to make the safe choice and not the easy one.

Mari turned, walked over to the doll, and gently picked it up. It was a ragdoll with yarn for hair and buttons for eyes, one of which was missing. It was very old, and it was obvious that it had been sewn by hand. Mari realized that Rose's mother had most likely sewn it and given it to her daughter.

Another crack of lightning brought Mari back to the present, and she quickly hurried inside. She took the doll to the sitting room that had a window seat. It was one of the other great spots in the house that looked out into the bay. She placed the doll on the seat and headed for the door.

As she closed and locked the door, Mari thought she heard the sound of footsteps on the wood floor and the faint sound of laughter.

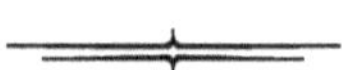

It took only a couple of days for Mari to receive an offer from the Niles's attorney for the property. They offered the exact asking price, and a couple of weeks later, the house was sold.

Six months later, a currier delivered a package to Mari. In it was a letter, business card, and a check.

Dear Ms. Scriller,

Enclosed please find a check that will more than adequately compensate you for the listing and sale of the house at 415 Mills St. My attorney's firm is at your disposal to assist you with anything you find necessary to have this transaction occur with the utmost speed.

The only thing I require, other than your discretion at the reason and nature of my wife's death, is that you again disclose the nature of the house and only allow the purchase to a buyer who understands the property's particular nuances and thus will treat it with the correct precaution.

If this deal is amicable, please reach out to my attorney. I have enclosed a card for your convenience.

Regards,

Robert Niles

Mari looked at the card, which had the name of the firm that had previously assisted the Niles in the closing. She then looked at the check, which made out for $50,000, more than three times what she would make on the sale of the house.

She placed the check on the table and picked up her phone to call the attorney. She needed to work out the details and get the keys.

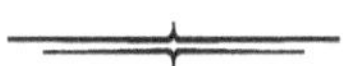

The house was on the market for less than two days when Mari got the first buyers wanting to look at the property. Mari pulled up to the curb to find the couple and their realtor already waiting.

As Mari approached, she painted the all too familiar smile on her face. "Hello. I am sorry if I am a couple minutes late." As she shook their hands, she tried to surmise if this visit would be worth the time. Their name was Moston, and they were both successful in the medical field.

Mari gave her normal spiel about the location and the different features of the house as they walked up the steps and into the house. When they walked through the sitting room, the realtor asked, "What is that?"

Rosey was right where Mari had left her.

Erika Lance

Erika had the unique opportunity to live in several different environments across the country growing up, giving her a colorful perspective on life. Born in Minnesota, she spent most of her formative years in Hollywood, then a ranch in New Mexico on the border of an Indian reservation. With a love of the arts since she was a child (acting, painting, sewing and dancing to name a few!) she found her passion in writing. Beginning with short stories, poems and articles for local papers, "Jimmy" is her first published fiction story.

More Erika Lance Books

Illusions of Happiness
No Place for Happiness

Jimmy

Jump: a horror novel
on the **YONDER** mobile app

Kait Disney-Leugers
Antique Magic
Blood Magic
Heart Magic

Lyra R. Saenz
Prelude
Sonata
Scherzo
Falsetto in the Woods: Novella
The Devil's Trill
Ragtime Swing
Midnight Cumbia
Sea Song De le Corsaire

Maria Devivo
Aestrangel the Fallen
Aestrangel the Chosen
Aestrangel the Risen

Megan Mackie
The Finder of the Lucky Devil
The Saint of Liars
The Devil's Day
The Digital Mage
The Lost
The Constable
Seath and the Crone

Paige Lavoie
I'm in Love with Mothman
I'm Engaged to Mothman

Robert J. Lewis
Shadow Guardian and the
Three Bears
Shadow Guardian and the
Big Bad Wolf
Shadow Guardian and the Boys
That Went Woof

Valerie Willis
Cedric: The Demonic Knight
Romasanta: Father of Werewolves
The Oracle: Keeper of the Gaea's Gate
Artemis: Eye of Gaea
King Incubus: A New Reign

Anthologies & Collections

Demonic Anthologies
Demonic Wildlife
Demonic Household
Demonic Carnival
Demonic Classics

Demonic Vacations
Demonic Medicine
Demonic Workplace
& more to follow!

Discover more at 4HorsemenPublications.com

www.ingramcontent.com/pod-product-compliance
Lightning Source LLC
Chambersburg PA
CBHW050158110726
47898CB00008B/2850